The Lost Blonde Anthology
on
EXISTENCE

The Lost Blonde Anthology
on
EXISTENCE

EDITED BY
Erin M. Arnold

A Lost Blonde Anthology

Introduction and selection © 2025 Lost Blonde, LLC

Cover Art: *Star Whisper* by Lisa Dailey

ISBN 979-8-9924345-3-8

10 9 8 7 6 5 4 3 2

Published by Lost Blonde Literary
www.lostblondelit.com

CONTENTS

POETRY

Paris Rosemont
> Endangered 7
> Spoons

Mary Ellen Shaughan
> Center Aisle, Fourth Pew from the Rear

Jonathan Ukah
> The Night I Saw the Moon

VISUAL ART

Lis Anna-Langston
> The Fables

Wesley R. Bishop
> Vulcan at Peace

Lisa Dailey
> Spring
> Bloom

Edward Lee
> Fire of Self
> Before You I Am
> Flight of Days

Welcome,

We find that people often focus on the meaning of life and that, in search of such a thing, it is often overlooked. That is—the beauty is in the beginning, the end, but mostly it is in everything in between. Our existence is the meat and meaning of our lives. We asked for artists to submit work to us based on whatever existence meant to them, as a result we received work that focused on birth, death, love, heartbreak, the stunning, and the absurd. We sincerely hope that you enjoy the collection contained in the following pages and that it encourages you to be fully present in your own existence and revel in the strength and beauty surrounding us all.

You may notice the omission of page numbers and I can assure you that this is deliberate. Peruse these artists at your leisure, and when you go back to find that one line or that one visual that resonated with you, you may find yourself revisiting the others that you forgot you loved as well.

One of the missions of Lost Blonde is to encourage creators of every art form to carry on. In cultivating this anthology, our editors were astounded by the number of moving pieces that were entrusted to us. Not all could be accepted, but in every work considered it was apparent that the creators had taken their soul to the page and sent it off to us. Whether accepted or not, we are so grateful that all this art, and all these artists, exist.

Best,
Erin M. Arnold

Michael Berton

Michael Berton has had poems appear in *Cold Noon, Sin Fronteras Journal, Shot Glass Journal, And/Or, Volt, The Opiate, Caveat Lector, Gargoyle, Fourteen Hills, El Portal, Yellow Medicine Review, Otoliths, Blaze Vox, Indefinite Space, The Blinking Cursor, Hinchas de Poesia, Caesura* and others. He was nominated for the Touchstone Award for Poetry in 2021. A poetry collection *Man! You Script the Mic.* came out in 2013 from Mitote Press. He lives in Portland, Oregon.

And Then There Were Those

---

that left no daily record
or followed any meticulous routine
committed no heinous crime
acquired no fortune
that left only a name
a few habitual belongings
in a run-down
one bedroom apt.
in a crime
ridden neighborhood

that had no soulmate
or fuck buddy
too aloof and weary
to procreate
a son or daughter
just a wanderlust
adrenalized in the body
that kept them mindful
of acknowledging themselves

that took no risks
never looked a second glance
that boogied no shake
shagged no carpet
fostered no addiction
followed no faith
or curiosity in the bland

who abbreviated their passions
raged no protest
mimicking the status quo quagmire
then who rested
when the rowing went upstream
whose madness
found a calming
in unraveling the future

then there are those
who became a thought
in a character's mind
or a persona in a poem
written by the anonymous
in a language
on its last print run
on the cusp
of being archived
in cyberspace

those that represented wealth
as their life's goal
feeding on money making
time from other people's lives
a gift to the world's misery
where currency markets never close
on a glimpse of immortality

and then there are those
who disregarded their inner music
hindering their ability
to dance alone
in a downtown
rush hour
while civilization
blared and bellowed
a cacophonous disapproval

Lis Anna-Langston, The Fables

B. J. Burton

B.J. Burton is a writer of plays, short stories, nonfiction, and poetry. She has had work published in *The Orchards Poetry Journal, Philadelphia Poets, Philly Fiction,* and elsewhere. As a produced and published playwright, her plays have been performed in Philadelphia, Pittsburgh, and New York. Honors include two fellowships from Pennsylvania Council on the Arts. Her MFA is from Rosemont College.

The Sneezing Man Who's Missing a Piece of His Jacket

Every time I ride the train and arrive at the Devon station, I see this man, a bit balding, gray hair with crinkles around his eyes, probably from laughing too much in sun, who sits basically in the same place and sneezes at exactly 8:02 a.m., not with a mild "ah-choo" but with a robust "kah-koosh," and it's so loud and unsettling that the other passengers have kept their distance, but I haven't because one time when I tripped in the aisle getting off at 30th Street, and all my books fell and scattered underneath the seats, and while the other passengers ignored me like they do, the sneezing man put down the Times and helped me locate all my books for this American Lit class I'm taking downtown, but what I noticed more than anything was that this little piece of fabric about one-inch square was dangling like a loose tooth from the back of his brown tweed jacket and looked like it needed to be pulled off so it would feel better, so as he was gathering up my books, I couldn't help but yank off that little wardrobe malady and stuff it in my own jacket pocket, where I've kept it mixed up with an old Trident wrapper for three months now, and I don't think he even misses it, but if he were to have, say a slightly disconnected button, I might find a way to grab that, too, and I'd keep those things together in my pocket and sit closer to him than anybody else on the whole entire train.

Zubayr Charles

Zubayr Charles is a multi-disciplinary writer who graduated
cum laude from UCT in Cape Town, South Africa with a
Master's in Creative Writing. As an emerging playwright and
director, his works — *Mercy*; *Please, don't call me moffie*; *The
Battered Housewives' Club*; and *this bra's a psycho* — have been
showcased at various theatres and festivals in Cape Town.
His essays are published on *LitNet* and *Cape Creative Collective*.
His poetry collection titled *the sad boy's starter pack* will be
released later this year and his first novel *Haram* is set to be
published early next year – both dealing with the theme of
queer identity.

The loquat tree

While trudging breathlessly in broken solitude,
I noticed a shadow of a loquat tree dancing
to the flickering of strobe light of the moon.

The towering tree snapped at my attention—
its golden oval eyes glaring into my hazy gaze.
So I stepped closer, intrigued by its beauty.

The glossy leaves and its shadow enticed me,
providing me with much needed shelter.
Intrigued. My glance to rolled over its dangling limbs.

I reached up at the oval eyes. My spoiled
fingertips clutching fiercely at the unknown.
In the process, I clenched too hard at the soft gold.

My hands were full of sticky sweet nectar,
encouraging me to lick my fingers and devour
the tangy juice. A taste so unfamiliar to me.

Quickly, I became addicted, gulping down
fruit after fruit. My stomach not getting full.
All I wanted was my heart to finally feel satisfied.

Insatiable. My hungry hands could not stop.
I wanted the loquat tree to show me affection, but
I knew that I needed to continue my journey home.

When I returned to the loquat tree, the sun revealed
bare and broken branches. How could others invade
the tree that I wanted. The tree belonged to me!

In the sunlight, I saw the loquat tree with clearer vision.
The rotten fruit lain on the floor spoiling my appetite. So,
I picked up one final fruit, even though it was not good for me.

Wesley R. Bishop, *Vulcan at Peace*

William Doreski

William Doreski has published three critical studies and several collections of poetry. His work has appeared in many print and online journals. He has taught at Emerson College, Goddard College, Boston University, and Keene State College. His most recent book is *Riding the Comet*. Visit him at williamdoreski.blogspot.com.

Saint Catherine Arrives

Not Saint Catherine of the wheel
but another, subtler version
strolls up our driveway to teach us
the ins and outs of blasphemy.

Touching stones for luck, naming
babies after religious figures,
talking to cats and dogs as if
they bore the image of deities.

Those are venial blasphemies.
More serious crimes are withholding
charity from the woman begging
outside the supermarket, her kids

lean with hunger, and listening
to preachers extol politicians
who are famous sexual offenders
and have amassed personal wealth

mainly to pay off their lawyers.
The winter looms broad and long,
parasitical with unkempt passions.
Snow-heaps along the highway

gather filth and debris. The saint
warns us about the thin ice
underfoot not only on ponds
but everywhere: black ice

the greatest threat, the depth
beneath it bottomless except
for the heap of discarded scripture
on which we may safely alight.

Dizzy as a Clown Show

The winsome poverty of age—
dust in the corners, tissues
crumpled on the bedside table.

The woodstove sneers and hisses.
The house groans, tired of me
and my purple and gray outlook.

If I lean deeply enough to see
the thermometer mounted outside
I get dizzy as a clown show.

You told me I'd age more quickly
than the tired and hollow birch
threatening to fall on the driveway.

I believed you, but the rasp of crows
assured me that evolution
hadn't entirely passed me by.

I drag the vacuum from its lair
and hoover up the ugliest dust.
The tissues wilt in the trash can.

Today I'll pack up all the books
I've read in the past year and sell
them to the bearded fellow

with a shop in his revamped garage.
I'm too old to reread anything
but the old newspapers I found

under the bed where the cats play
in the innocence of all furred things,
their futures too distant to touch.

Lisa Dailey, *Spring*

Nadine Ellsworth-Moran

Nadine Ellsworth-Moran lives in Georgia where she works in full-time ministry while pursuing her love of writing. She hopes to continue listening closely and writing about the shared experience of life in these times, with particular interest in the joys and struggles of coming to understand the history, identity, faith, and culture of the modern South. Her poems have appeared in *McNeese Review, The Brussels Review, Theophron, Rust + Moth, Thimble, Sonic Boom, Emrys, Kakalak,* and *The Wild Word,* among others. She shares her home with her husband and five unrepentant cats.

Fly Casting

We cannot reel back the wind
that has swum by so unceremoniously,
so we set our hooks, baited with shiny
lures in hopes of a speckled breeze.

It would be easier with nets,
I suppose. Still, there are too many holes—
and all the small obscurities will sieve
through delicate as cake flour

and sift down to settle in the floorboards
where we can never retrieve them.
We may try with an arsenal of tools,
searching out each reluctant grain.

But this could take years
and we are hardly archeologists.
I thought we were fishermen.
Either way, the waiting is the same.

Samuel Lorraine Goldsmith

Samuel Lorraine Goldsmith (he/him) is a former musician who lives in California with his family. He writes so as to be a river, not a lake. His writing has appeared or is forthcoming in *82 Review, Gone Lawn, Gyroscope*, and others.

Family Health History

Hi. Just responding to your text. You're probably in physical therapy right now. I'll try and keep this short, but you know me. I'll probably go right up to the limit again. Oh, I wish I wasn't like this, but it's as Bernstein as baldness or hairy arms or getting hangry. Nothing to be done.

Anyway. The long and short of it is, I don't know the answer to your doctor's question. You told her about my heart attack, right? Does she really need to know the circumstances? Not quite the same thing that happened to you, so. It's kind of embarrassing, but, I don't know, call me back if you want the whole story. I mean, I wasn't doing much when it happened. You know I do that walk every day. Used to. Whatever. Just call me.

I did some digging into your grandparents. Not much there, sorry. Not just that they never told anyone anything, another Bernstein thing, but they didn't spend much time in doctor's offices. Part of growing up poor, huh. Papa, I remember he banged up his foot at the factory once. He used to limp around everywhere. He and Nana, they just waited. That was their plan, just to wait. Well, then it swelled up to the size of a football and stretched out his shoes. I swear, that man never agreed to see a doctor unless he was at death's door. So then, he finally went and they rushed him into surgery. Kept him there a couple days. They asked why he waited so long. I know what he thought. They're all quacks. There's no reason to see a doctor except to get meds. Yes, I know. He was stubborn as you and me and all us Bernsteins, but. Listen. You have to remember where he came from. That factory town in the Rust Belt. Never even heard of a big city doctor, like yours.

Sorry, I'm rambling. But I need to tell you. I love you. I don't say it enough. They'll figure out what's wrong with you, and you'll get through this. I love…

The Doubtlessness Test

There comes a time when a person knows everything there is to know about the world, when the globe keeps spinning without them. Curiosity launches interstellar and all that remains on earth is the certainty that nothing else is as it should be. The quantities of some things are too high, while those of others are too low.

Most reach this point without realizing it. One day they wake up weightless of mystery or wonder. Unconcerned how far those parts of themselves have fled.

There exists a simple test, fashioned by a famous German doctor now known best for his unflinching support of the Nazi regime, to determine whether you belong to this doubtless group. It goes like this. First, make sure you are seated with model posture. Both feet should be planted on the floor, footwear optional. Now, lift your non-dominant foot. Keep it aloft for the duration of the test.

Next comes a series of questions. Answer only those which apply to you. When was it that your mother suffered most, and what was the cause? Was it when you and your brother tracked twiggy snow through the house on your rubber outdoor boots, shrieking with the thrill of the chase; or when it was just you, shrieking alone? How about when she bolted out the door without so much as a scarf around her neck, breath white on the air, down to the shard-surfaced lake? Which god was it she saw when she planted her knees on the frigid shore? How many gold coins did she claw from the muck? How long did it take you to realize this entire string of questions was nothing but a metaphor? You never had a brother, not a real one, not one you could trust with your life, did you? Did you infer that the brother in these questions drowned? Why? Is it because your mother really did suffer, really did wish it was you instead who died? When was it that you came to understand your life to be the bare needles in everyone else's mattresses?

Now: is your non-dominant foot still aloft?
If you have attained doubtlessness, you know what the answer means.

The Unreliable Narrator is Overly Self-Critical

The title calls me an unreliable narrator, but I'm more of an unreliable person. Can't be trusted with a secret, because who knows when you'll see it next. Can't be counted on to show up on time. Give me a deadline at your own risk. Birthdays? Point me to the "Sorry I Missed It" cards. I'm the type to forget to bring bait to a fishing trip, a dish to a potluck, a plastic bag to walk the dog.

Actually, all that's not completely true. I'll keep your secret. My mind will change it into something other than what it was, give it a membrane of misremembering to hide in. Like when your brand of bread was out of stock and you screamed at me and chucked the stand-in I'd bought, then screamed at me again the next time when I came back empty-handed. By the time I venture to release your screams from my mouth as words, they will carry only regret that I made you upset, and shame at my inability to do a simple thing. And even if I could reveal your secret, nobody would bother to believe me. After all, I'm an unreliable person.

Edward Lee, Fire of Self

John Grey

John Grey is an Australian poet, US resident, recently published in *New World Writing, City Brink* and *Tenth Muse*. Latest books, *Subject Matters, Between Two Fires* and *Covert* are available through Amazon. He also has work upcoming in *Hawaii Pacific Review, Amazing Stories*, and *Cantos*.

Another Day at the Assisted Living Facility

Once again, Josie is speechless.
No commentary. A woman
is too young to die, even at 87.
She appears to casually prepare
the room for the next one
but all she can do is whisper,
"Nothing can be done."
She's shaken, instinctively prays.
The silence is overwhelming,
from the empty bed to the
alabaster bathroom. And the
glass, the metal, she shines,
even the edges of a single cup—
all reveal her tortured face.
A small writing desk, flowers—
anything to give false comfort
to the dying. It didn't work.
The handkerchiefs are folded,
the nightdress forsaken.
Every last item that belonged
to the dead woman has been
too long in grief.
The only life is Josie's now.
She feels unfit to occupy it

"Stay alive? For what?
To indulge myself in
senseless, endless movement?"
She remembers the dead woman.
Martha was her name: wrinkled
brow, shiny drooping cheeks,
but eyes round and pale-bright
as day-moons. Now it's just
rooms, spaces awaiting its
people. The last one is
already lost forever.
There is little talk in the corridors.
Everyone who works here
from the doctors and nurses
to the cleaning crew are
resigned to death. The indifferent
faces are merely showmanship.
This is the law after all—
to suffer, to waste away.
That's why these people are here.
Some sit. Some eat.
But none can do it for themselves.
So why does the tree
continue to bear fruit
when it knows the soul's last stand
is in a wretched, aging body?
A mop and bucket is the only answer.

Lola J. Hobson

Lola Hobson is a writer/poet based in the North of Wales where she studies English Literature. Her work has been featured in Wingless Dreamer's *Echoes of Frost and Fantasies* anthology, as well as on the PoetryFest blog, and Bangor University's English Instagram page.

The Snow

The snow didn't feel right. It was wrong. It wasn't wrong in the way snow might feel at the end of March, nor was it wrong in feeling too wet. It was wrong in its bones, if snow had bones. It fell in tiny little circles that seemed too perfect for it to be a coincidence. The snow caught the light, it glistened in a way that made the air ache in pain. *The snow is always like this*, I told myself. Deep down, I knew I was lying to myself.

My younger sister and I always used to make snow angels, *hadn't we?* I could picture the outlines of our limbs sprawled across the white blanket that suffocated our lawn and our flower beds. The memory felt sticky. Sticky like a sweet that had been left unwrapped on the counter for too long. I tried to picture her face, the way she threw her head back when she laughed, throwing handfuls of powdery white at me. My mind fogged up with the image of an old swing set against the pale sky. The swings were void of children playing, a large pile of snow sat on each of the two seats.

On the wind, tunes that sounded like the lullabies my mum sang in my childhood, chimed. The words sounded blurry, and I couldn't make them out. I tried to hum along to one of the softer tunes, but it slipped through my lips like the watery soup my mum used to make.

"This is how the winters were," I murmur, no one was there to agree or disagree. The shape of the lie on my lips felt nice, it curled in my mouth like a mint. It tasted sharp and exciting.

The snow fell faster, it piled up in strange and angled piles. *Why does it never melt?* I pondered. The sun had borne down on the Earth all afternoon, my skin was red and flaky from being burned by the ferocious rays of light. My fingers hadn't stung when I touched the baby powdered grass, they didn't sting like I thought they would. It was electric, my fingers hummed as I reached for a handful of snow. Static. It was a lullaby in itself. Not stinging. Exciting. It was like a mound of those small peppermints with the hole in the middle, only if they'd been left unwrapped near the hob long enough to have gone soft, or soggy.

I knelt down shakily, my knees dented the snow, and I could no longer see them as they buried themselves deeper and deeper, my trousers getting soaked and then I couldn't feel my knees at all. I tried to make a snowball. The snow compressed together obediently, like a memory you wanted to remember forever. It was warm in my hands, and heavy. *It isn't supposed to be like this.* I shuddered. I didn't know why I thought it was wrong, I couldn't remember.

The frozen pond in my garden looked like a shattered mirror, similar to the one I had thrown at my sister in a rage after she stole something from me, I couldn't remember what she had stolen. I had never skated on the pond before, yet I could feel the blades as they scraped across the ice, I could hear the grating sound. I shuddered. Cold air brushed against my cheeks, but it felt warm. *It isn't supposed to be like this.* The memory fit me snugly. *It wasn't mine.*

The snow whispered and laughed, its voice was soft, like a kitten. So soft that it wasn't understandable. Maybe it wasn't the snow after all. Maybe it was me. *It isn't supposed to be like this.* Remembered wrong? Perhaps I'd never lived this. But the snow was wrong, *yes*, that was the only possible thing. The snow had to be wrong. I sat down; the polystyrene-like texture drowned me as it sang the blurry songs of my childhood. *The Snow was wrong.*

It isn't supposed to be like this.

The snow.

Wrong.

It was wrong.

Thomas Mantz, *Porto #1*

Nancy Byrne Iannucci

Nancy Byrne Iannucci is a librarian and poet who lives with her two cats: Nash and Emily Dickinson. *THRUSH Poetry Journal, Allegro Poetry Magazine, Eunoia, Maudlin House, San Pedro River Review, 34 Orchard, Bending Genres, Discretionary Love,* and *Typehouse,* are some places you will find her. She is the author of four chapbooks: *Temptation of Wood* (Nixes Mate Review, 2018), *Goblin Fruit* (Impspired, 2021), *Primitive Prayer* (Plan B Press, fall 2022), and *Hummingbirds and Cigarettes* (Bottlecap Press, 2024). Visit her at www.nancybyrneiannucci.com.

Just as They Were About to Bloom

We are going to Italy in March. *Italy in March* – sings like *April in Paris:* Eros Ramazzotti will fill the air as we float up the Piazza di Spagna. And there, my lover will kiss me and when the time is right, he will say to me in his shaky Italian, *È ora, amore mio, di far visita a mio padre – (it's time, my love, to visit my father)* who is buried at the Basilica di Santa Maria in Montesanto, known as the *Church of Artists.* His father was a painter, a dreamy man, who had the look of a blended Claude Monet and Walt Whitman. I wanted to meet this man who made my lover. I wanted to see the similarities and differences. His mother said they had the same eyes, but he passed away before our trip like the sickly child who died in the sky, just after treatment, dying before she could get better. And the figure skaters who died above the icy Potomac, fit for the gold but dying before they could feel its weight around their necks. I curse this moment; the evil interval that snatches life like the frost that took the buds on my magnolia tree just as they were about to bloom.

Maggie Nerz Iribarne

Maggie Nerz Iribarne is a 55-year-old woman, lives in Syracuse, NY, writes about witches, priests/nuns, the very, very old, struggling teachers, neighborhood ghosts, and whatever else strikes her fancy. She keeps a portfolio of her published work at www.maggienerziribarne.com.

Might be a Murderer

Even then, when I was so little, I feared him. He held me in sunshine beside the linden tree in front of my mother's rental. Sometimes his lips came close to my ear and he kissed me, leaving saliva on my cheek. I waited for him to turn before I wiped his residue away.

*****

"Everyone says he's weird, that he looks at them funny. All my girlfriends do. I know what they mean," I said.

My mother clipped coupons. Her cigarette burned in an ashtray. "He's not *that* weird. He's just, like, a nerd. He's on the spectrum, I think."

I was twelve by this time. I never told my mother the truth, that he'd put his hand under my bottom when I sat down, more times than I could count, telling me he liked to feel my blubber, my extra padding.

Every Friday, he showed up for dinner and Mom put on a nice blouse and perfume and made him a ziti. Then he slept with her, in her room. I made sure I had other plans those nights.

***

At Patti's and other friends' homes, I saw what real nerdy fathers were like. They smiled, ruffled their daughters' hair, called them Sweets, Pattikins. Their daughters rolled their eyes at them in annoyance, embarrassment over dumb jokes and strict rules. Everyone avoided any mention of my father. It was always, "How's your mom?" and "You're always welcome, here, Candy." Pity rained down in the forms of comments and invitations, by softened eyes and downturned mouths.

Once, Patti and I had a séance. She called forth the spirits of the dead.

"Let's try to bring that college student, Maria Winters, back. Let's try to get her to tell us who her murderer was."

"Maria who?" I said, legs folded beneath me, hands spread out on my knees meditation style, my back straight as a stick.

"Maria-the girl they found strangled in the dorm," Patti said it flat and matter-of-factly, like she was ordering at a restaurant.

"I don't know. I never-"

Patti's voice dissolved into my crowding thoughts, racing heart.

"What's up?" she said.

"I feel. I feel like. I don't know. I'm scared. Like something like that could happen to me."

"Well, yeah, right? It could happen to anybody."

Patti pulled out a beer from under her bed, cracked the tab.

***

Before my father disappeared, my life felt like a roller coaster creeping, creeping, creaking to some unknown precipice which would end in a violent, terrifying swoop to a merciless ground. When he stopped showing up on Fridays, the roller coaster stopped, brakes slammed, sun overhead baking into my defenseless skin. That was a new kind of terror altogether.

***

Sophomore year of college a girl on my campus was murdered in her dorm room. Beaten, then strangled.

"Who does that?" my roommate Zoe asked, as though she was asking something low-key disturbing, like who puts mayo on spaghetti. My mind went blank at first, then a disgusting sickness rose up inside me. I'd never forgotten the girl Patti tried to raise from the dead during our séance. My heart began its wild drumbeat. Something in my head clicked into place.

My father, I wanted to say. *My father would do that. My father does that.*

The thought formed and it wouldn't fade.

I hadn't seen him in years, but still I googled my father's name repeatedly, trying to connect him with some crime, searching fruitlessly until hitting someone who matched my exploding fear: Ted Bundy.

Ted had a method.

He pretended to have a broken leg, asked some poor, about-to-be-murdered college girl for help. She'd agree, then he'd drag her off and beat her to death. He killed at least 30 women this way, probably way more, and even his long-term girlfriend didn't suspect. I held an old photo of my father up against the glowing computer screen, his and Ted's faces blurring together.

***

First, I walked briskly along the sidewalk, avoiding eye contact, moving from dorm to cafeteria to classroom and back. Then I was afraid to go out, afraid to talk to guys, to anyone, afraid to leave the window open, unlocked. I cut off all my hair. Ted crawled through windows, preferred girls with long hair.

"Why don't you just go home?" Zoe asked, "You don't seem very happy here."

I didn't want to tell her about my home, my father who could appear there any minute. Instead, I scheduled online classes, ordered food delivery, hid out in my room.

Zoe called Mental Health Services.

Mental Health Services called my mother.

***

"No! No!" I screamed, spitting, flailing. My mother grabbed my shoulders.

"Candy! What in God's name?"

I kicked and bit. "How could you? How could you?"

"How could I what?"

"How could you choose him?"

"Who?"

"Dad! Ted! Ted Bundy?" I slid backwards in the bed, straight and staring like a corpse.

"Ted Bundy?" she sat down, lifted a glass of water to my lips.

My attention drifted to a man standing at my door.

"He's here! That's. That's him!"

"No, honey, that's Matthew, the counselor."

I looked from his face to hers. Back and forth. Sweat trickled from my hairline.

My mother wiped my brow.

"I got myself together, Candy. I got a new job, stopped drinking. I'm doin' better."

"But what about him? Did you know he's here?"

"Who?"

"My father. Ted Bundy."

"Your father isn't Ted Bundy."

"Yes, yes he is."

"*No.* Ted Bundy is dead. Your father is Patrick Gravels and he's living in Fort Lauderdale with his cousin. He works at a liquor store, I think. He's not a murderer."

She smoothed my spikey hair.

"But how do you know? How do you know for sure?" I screamed over and over, so many times, until my throat was raw.

She never gave me a good answer, never, not once.

Michael Moreth, *Germinate*

Stephen Joffe

Stephen Joffe is an award-winning actor, musician, writer, and sound designer based in Toronto. He has previously been published as a playwright, songwriter (Birds of Bellwoods, etc.), and poet. His publications in 2025 include *Humber Literary Review*, *Squid Lit Magazine*, *The Scop*, *Willows Wept Review*, *Lost Blonde*, *Amethyst Review*, *Pinhole Poetry*, *Dalhousie Review*, *Chrysalism*, *The Pointed Circle*, and more.

THERE IS NO BLACK HORSE

---

death is not a catch
neither punishment, nor judgement
& not something   to worry about: for

                    she will come, & perfectly on time.

bearing strange gifts
        you do not recognize:
turning old pains   to treasures
                    heavy, heavy in their tearful gild.

& now, she stands before me
i must accept
        that there are no
        uninvited guests   here—

i simply   was not ready for company.

she has your hand   that was always hers—
you are only going   to the other room.

there is no black horse.

only memories,   & plants to water.

Janina Aza Karpinska

Award-winning poet, Janina Aza Karpinska, achieved an M.A. in Creative Writing & Personal Development, with Merit, at Sussex University. Drawing on many influences, and writing in a variety of styles, her work has appeared in *Poems in the Waiting Room; London Reader; Magma; Ekphrastic Review; Sein und Werden; Epistemic Lit; Drawn to the Light; Heron Tree; Cold Signal; Synchronized Chaos,* and *Raising the Fifth,* amongst others. She lives on the south coast of England.

Upstaged

Baby clings to mama's neck, but
mum's distracted – mind elsewhere,
turning from smell of milk, baby-fat,
heat-on-skin; arms pulled tight; spit-up;
choking, with no escape from this
all-consuming need (bar sporadic,
broken sleep).

'Wardrobe' reduced to a robe the colour of
bleeds she no longer has. Dry and brittle
hair, uncared for; bare face, no make-up;
her own needs displaced in this new role
as 'extra', where she'd once been top
of the bill. A star in her own drama.

Now Baby's stolen the show: mini-diva-
cum-director, with her very own 'dresser'.

'What baby wants, baby gets'
is written into the contract. Mum knows
this will run and run for the longest time.

Baby hangs on for all she's worth;
and no-one, at any time, says:

'Cut!'

Medicine

As in *hair of the dog that bit* –
being the thing that brings relief;
the way homeopathic remedies work,
where the hint of caffeine in *caffea*
is used to treat insomnia. Just so,

take solitude to combat loneliness,
time alone – by choice and purpose.

Turn *upset* into the thing that sets you up
after you've been knocked down; you're not
'out for the count' (if you know *you* count).
A negative has its positive opposite when
flipped on its axis; perspective switched.

So take the pitchfork sticking in your ribs,
and pitch a synopsis - your tale of pain
and betrayal could become the next
prize-winning novel. No joke –

turn the dog ends of life to dogged application;
snifff out new trails that lead to success; deep
breaths, and new beginnings; expanded chest,
filled with pride; not a dead loss, then, but alive.

Avril's Wake

A feast of sandwiches and remembrances,
sausages and chat, crisps and intimate whispers,
an *awful* lot of salad in resealable plastic boxes;
small cakes and potted anecdotes, risqué jokes,
cheese on cocktail sticks, and stories that
couldn't be told in chapel. *God!*

She loved food: had bought a juicer to extract
the utmost from fruit and veg; gave all she met
packs of brown rice and advice at the jazz club
she frequented with hi-camp Reg. *Oh!*

She knew what was good to eat, alright, but
also loved a treat; secrets always revealed
by chocolate-smeared fingers and lips,
and the empty wrappers at her feet.

Camellia Paul, *Hairer*

E. D. Lloyd-Kimbrel

New Jersey native and New England resident E. D. Lloyd-Kimbrel (whose car masquerades as a branch library) has been writing for a while. Over the years, in between various employments and educational endeavors, geographical locations and life events, she has published biographical, critical, and scholarly articles and essays in academic arenas along with poems and creative non-fiction in literary ones. Her debut poetry chapbook, *Matrimonies*, was released from the starting gate by Finishing Line Press in summer 2023.

Field Trip

Aaron had been my boyfriend, as much as a girl in the third grade can have a boyfriend. Boyfriends were then judged by how many insults they slung at certain girls. I had received quite a share. So, I don't see why Amy cried so much. He hadn't been her boyfriend. He'd never even said "boo" to her. I didn't cry at all.

It was the first day back at school after spring vacation and we were outside for morning recess, except Aaron was absent. I was in mid-toss for hopscotch when Amy got hysterical. Amy was like that—missing her jump-in for double dutch could bring on weeping. Supposedly her mother was an ogre, although she seemed nice enough whenever I went over to Amy's house. Anyway, we all felt sorry for Amy. We were also jealous of her because she was filthy rich and had perfect hair. Amy's best friend told us what had happened: Aaron and his family had a car accident while on vacation; Aaron was the only one seriously hurt; he had been in the hospital, and everyone had thought he was getting better when he had just dropped dead one night.

We were silent for a minute or so—Amy quietened down since she didn't want to attract any teacher's attention—and then we went back to playing until the bell rang.

After school I waited on the corner a full fifteen minutes—that was according to my new wristwatch, which my parents had gotten me so I'd know how long I dawdled—until I remembered that Aaron was dead and wouldn't be there to insult me today.

The next day at the beginning of class our teacher announced we were going over to the funeral home for the "visiting hours" so we could say good-bye to our classmate. It was also the day of class pictures so we were all already dressed nicely.

The few blocks walk to the funeral home was like any other class outing: double file with partners holding hands. The line was broken periodically by someone distracted by a cat or squirrel or tree limb. With my partner I played "step on a crack and break a witch's back." We'd changed the rhyme from "your mother's back" because we loved our mothers and didn't want any mistake to hurt them. But we felt sympathetic towards witches too and so tried not to step on too many cracks. The sidewalk was slate slabs with lots of cracks from heaves because of tree roots shouldering through. The teacher kept telling us to shush and we kept making lots of noise.

When we got to the funeral home the teacher stopped us outside. She explained that this was a place of mourning, of sadness, that Aaron's relatives were in there, and that we were to be very quiet and just walk past the casket and come outside again. Someone had the gumption to ask what a casket was, and the teacher started to say something about a bed but was interrupted by someone else who said "it's a box like you bury your pet mouse in." That sobered everyone up.

I remember the funeral home felt cluttered and smelled funny. It was like somebody's house, with a staircase and rooms off the hallway, so calling it a home seemed valid. Flowers were everywhere but the air held something besides the heavy floral scents, something like the musty smell old houses have when they haven't been opened for a long while. But there was another smell, a faint biting one, under the other smells, and I didn't like it.

We went down a narrow hall and then turned a corner into a large thick-carpeted room. Here there were even more flowers and also candles, all lit even though it was daytime, and people in dark clothes. They were standing in groups or sitting alone, and I don't remember their faces. It seemed as if they didn't have any faces. We could see Aaron was at the far end of the room in what we guessed was the casket. I remember thinking how stupid our single file passing through must have looked to all those dark, blank people.

Aaron himself looked sort of asleep and sort of grumpy, surrounded by soft cushiony satin, like some pillows I'd seen at Amy's house. So, it was kind of a bed as well as a box. Aaron didn't look like Aaron, though, dressed up in a suit and necktie. Aaron hated to get dressed up; he never liked having to spiff for class picture day. And his freckles, his freckles were barely there. Aaron wasn't Aaron without his freckles. They'd done something powdery to his face. I might have said something then but the line kept moving and I was gently shuttled out of the room and through the front door and down the porch steps to the sidewalk.

Some of the girls were teary because it seemed the thing to do. Amy was absent for some reason, so she'd missed the class pictures as well, and she loved having her picture taken. Once we were out of earshot of the funeral home we went back to being somewhat unruly but also somewhat subdued. I felt no sense of sorrow, not then anyway. There was an unease I couldn't explain, but mainly I was just glad to get away from the strange smell and also that long division had been relegated to another day thanks to class pictures and Aaron.

After school that afternoon I waited on the corner, for half an hour this time, before walking on home. I knew Aaron wouldn't appear. Maybe it was a tribute, an instinct or something, waiting that long. As I clumped into the house my mom called from the kitchen with her usual question, "What did you do at school today?"

"We went on a field trip," I answered.

"Oh? That's news." There was a pause, "where to?"

Edward Michael Supranowicz, *The Absurdity of it All*

Prue King

Prue King's published short stories and poetry appear in recent anthologies (such as *Everyday Fiction, London Grip and Tarot*), a parenting book for new dads, and stage plays. She studied writing for the theatre in Houston and has half an arts degree. Prue lives in the luxuriant far north of New Zealand with a head full of words.

---

a bunch of white flowers

I heard the big mare stomp a hoof as we came into the turn. She'd been standing still for almost two hours, her tiny foal resting under her in the hay on the horse float floor. Ahead the road forked, the right veering back into the hills and the left, ours, to the plains of the valley. In between was an enormous oak tree that had witnessed horse, cart and motorised traffic for a century and hard into its unforgiving trunk was a freshly mangled ute, 'Joe Wright, Farrier', still readable on the side panel.

Three bystanders kept vigil on the grass, not close to the vehicle, but on watch still. We gently pulled over and a woman, clad all in white, drifted across the road to us, her hands locked together.

'He's dead. The driver's dead.'

'No, that's awful.'

'He must have come round that corner and headed straight for the tree. He had two roads to choose from and look what happened. How did he do that?'

'The poor man. Are you sure he's dead?'

'He's dead alright. He won't be feeling any pain now.'

'Have you checked if anyone else was in there with him?'

'There's no-one. We're waiting here for the police.'

She sniffed, dabbed her eyes with a finger inside a fine white handkerchief and looked at me. 'We've been looking forward to lunch at the winery for weeks.'
We waved dismally and headed up the road. It was only another eight kilometres to the stud, but it could have been hours as we mulled over what had happened and why it had.

Why did the driver not avoid the tree? Should we turn around?

The front gates of the stud were wide, set back for delivery trucks and horse transports. We parked and lowered the ramp and led the mare from the float, she alerts with head high, her filly keeping close on stilted legs.

A stud worker took the mare to the teaser, then with the foal safely secured behind a barrier in the corner of the serving barn, they put the dam into the crush, twitched and hobbled her, wrapped her tail and washed her. Immediately there was a trumpeting from outside, crunching gravel and calming voices as the stallion pranced into the barn. His shaft like a fence post, he sniffed the mare, raised his nose into the air and curled back his top lip. He mounted her, thrust, head low, his body lying prone on her, finished as if dead. He calmly backed off; the mare stood still.

'Reckon that was a fair go,' said the stallion handler. 'I'd be surprised to see her back here this season. A bit like poor Joe, but he won't be coming back to work at all.'

We led the mare and foal to a day yard, gave them hay and had a quiet coffee in the lunchroom. After a break we loaded the horses for our silent journey home. The cops had put a tape around the gouged oak tree but the ute and its contents had gone.

A bunch of white flowers rested on the jagged grass.

Claudia Tong, *Vitality*

Zoé Mahfouz

Zoé Mahfouz is a multi-talented French artist: an award-winning bilingual Actress, Screenwriter, Content Creator, and Writer whose work spans fiction, nonfiction, and poetry. Her writing has appeared in over 70 literary magazines and best-of anthologies worldwide, including *Cleaver Magazine*, *OPEN: Journal of Arts & Letters*, *NUNUM*, as well as *Ginyu Magazine*, a respected journal of avant-garde and contemporary poetry, and *The Asahi Shimbun*, one of Japan's largest newspapers. While her fiction is often described as "very tongue-in-cheek," "kookie," and "random," her poetry, which ranges from seventeenth-century eerie Japanese haiku and haibun to more classical forms and the occasional ekphrastic poem, draws on anthropological strangeness and sharp mythological references. In contrast, her other poetic and prose works lean into a darker, more introspective register. They weave fragmented narrative with sensory overload and philosophical undercurrent, exploring themes such as psychiatric care, neurodivergence, and the collapse of identity.

Welcoming the New Male Employees

Hello, boys! And please, do not start complaining already with your "we are not boys, we are men." "Men" is a title that is not given in advance; it needs to be earned. A few ground rules need to be established before you start working for the company. First things first, no one wants to see you wearing those tight jeans or gym shirts because not only is it distracting for everyone, but it is also very likely to lead to HR complaints from you using big words like "sexual harassment," which is frankly ridiculous. We are all humans here and fully entitled to enjoy a fine toy when we see one, so ask yourself the right questions before waving all that testosterone around us.

Speaking of testosterone, I know hormones are a very big deal for you. Sometimes your tummy will hurt, you will be cranky, you will want children, blah blah blah, we know the drill, and we do not care. Take an aspirin. Control yourself. And do not even think about calling in sick because I will personally visit you and conduct a full palpation, even though the closest I have ever been to being a doctor was when I dressed as one for Halloween.

Also, I know you all get very excited about juicy gossip and "kiss, marry, kill" games, but chit-chat is not allowed at work, in the hallways, in the elevators, in the cafeteria, or in the bathroom. Yes, in the bathroom. And we will know if you break that rule because we have tiny cameras in there following your every move. Oh, and it is three sheets of toilet paper per employee per day, and stop pretending you need to sit down to pee. It is absurd. Learn to squat. You will all benefit from this workout considering you are all above the body mass index.

Speaking of which, each workday starts with what we call the "Lard of the Rings Test," where we weigh each employee, and the fattest person in the room gets to wear Dumbo ears for the entire day and becomes the target of the food battle at lunch. It is a fun team-building exercise. We are actually very proud to have lost eighteen employees this year to anorexia and even got this achievement framed in the *Guinness Book of World Records*.

If any of this confuses you, do not hesitate to ask a female employee for guidance, but choose your moment carefully: not before she has had her coffee, not while she is working, and not while she is on a break. Always assume she is doing something much more important and technical than you are, so try to be relevant and keep your eyes down when you talk to her. Learn her eating habits and greet her in the morning with a hot coffee and a few snacks. Just kidding. You are the snack.

Wear perfume, but not too much. Do not speak too loudly; it is always annoying and just shows us that you still do not know your place. If you are a good boy, they might even pat you on the head, which is the ultimate sign that you have made it.

Any questions? Of course not. You will need way more time than most people to process that amount of information. No, do not go there, boy! The conference room is for grown-ups! You do not start until this afternoon, so why not go kill time at the Sephora next door? Or go do your nails? Whatever it is that you do. And please, exit through the service door. The main building entrance also needs to be earned.

Now roll down your pants and kiss my feet.

Lisa Dailey, *Bloom*

DS Maolalai

DS Maolalai has been described by one editor as "a cosmopolitan poet" and another as "prolific, bordering on incontinent". His work has been nominated thirteen times for Best of the Net, ten for the Pushcart Prize, and once for the Forward Prize. He has released in three collections; *Love is Breaking Plates in the Garden* (Encircle Press, 2016), *Sad Havoc Among the Birds* (Turas Press, 2019), and *Noble Rot* (Turas Press, 2022).

Blue Barely Silhouette

every day he's out there. was a porter
once I think. drinks eight cans
in six hours, putting empties
in a plastic bag carefully.
looks at the fruit market.
the building is falling down
well. it could be a photograph.
isn't one. isn't a tattoo.
he leans against the bike stands
which never have bikes on them.
collapses like a building
in the dublin city centre near my house
and the shut fegans cafe.
old tattoos on skin fade
from detail to blue barely
silhouette. sometimes you can see
what something was.

Changeable

snow's swept to corners.
no longer falling;
just ice in a pile
in the doors outside shops
like a dirty sheet
next to a laundry basket.
I walk from the quayside
and uphill toward stoneybatter.
our fridge almost empty –
I'm going for groceries
late. and evening turns night-time
without any sunset
of colour. a page being placed
on a half-working lampshade –
a door closing softly;
unlit attic rooms. ahead of me
buses stop, heavy and hesitant
as a stag in a dark
fall of snow. passengers
exit, pushing hands
to the warm wells
of pockets. it was sunny
this morning – the day
has been changeable
weather. they shiver, puff shoulders
up into their jackets,
as if such a small thing is of help.

Leaving Tallaght

the blue secret eye of the sky
to the west and the evening.
this end of the city –
land scratched by developers
building brick wall to plasterboard
by highways, old bottlebanks and undeveloped
farmland. leaving tallaght, you pass fag-
end housing estates, groceries
backed onto petrol stations. in between, the trees bend
as if holding the clouds for a moment – a favour
they owe to the sky. the road here is broken
by traffic which passes, but not enough
to justify repair. a coworker shows
me a video of something
from his blessington housing
estate near the lakes and the mountain.
it's a man breaking into a van
and another man beating him
until blood comes out. pausing for breath
for a moment with shirt off
on what must be cold winter evening –
then checking to see if it's murder. you can see his breath
even on the bad cctv. eddie knows both – they drink
in the same pub sometimes. there are cities
and wilderness, edges of cities. traffic thickens
and thins out in evenings:
low tides making islands
and wandering crabs between trash.

Edward Lee, Before You I Am

Gargi Mehra

Gargi Mehra works in IT and moonlights as a creative writer. Her work has appeared in numerous literary magazines, including *Crannog, The Forge Literary Magazine, The Writer,* and others. She lives in Pune, India with her husband and two children. She blogs at www.gargimehra.com.

The Shape-Shifter and the Invisible Man

Under the watchful embers of a crackling *agni,* they pledge their vows. She longs to circle the holy flame in double-quick time, but the dhoti-clad, ash-smeared priest curbs her pace.

Don't rush for dinner, he says, and cackles in her face.

She contains her scowl, trailing her soon-to-be-husband with measured steps. It's like the pandit has drawn them into an orbit in slow motion. The man ahead of her, the deflowerer of her freedom, faxes no expression to his face. Midway through the *pheras,* the priest halts their turns about the holy fire. He instructs her to lead and reties the knot that links her shimmering stole to his. Her beau winks at her.

The morning after, she becomes an octopus, one deft hand slipping balls of dough into a vat of hot oil and another dicing spuds and another setting seven cups of water to boil for tea.

The man turns translucent, but his shine fades a little at a time.

When the sun hangs overhead, the newly minted shape-shifter morphs into a whale, skimming the ocean floor of her new home with her belly. She deprives the house of the dust that has veneered upon it, but it leaves her limp. After dark, her beau demands she stretch her limbs like a gazelle, but she longs to morph into a praying mantis and adopt their post-coital ritual.

All this while, the man begins to pale like the colours on a shade card.

Soon she waddles like a pachyderm, gestating for longer than anyone else. Months later she is a clownfish, jetting out a screaming pink creature.

Even when salt colours his hair more than pepper, he remains ethereal, disappearing soon after sunrise and arriving only after moonset. Eventually, his beloveds see right through him.

Only when he retires does the invisible man emerge once more and witness his shape-shifter wife morph into a turtle.

After She Left

We wrestled her nightgowns and her midis into fraying suitcases. We bickered over the digital slabs of metal she owned, and we locked up her guitar, because we knew she would never retrace her steps back to our hearth.

She had never catered to our heart's desires.

She'd never whipped up scrambled eggs, stacked our laundry into little block towers, airplane-landed morsels of curry-rice into our mouths, lighted candlewicks on Diwali, flash-flooded water into our bottles, lined up carrot sticks in our lunchboxes, stuffed our little feet into too-snug shoes, or even plopped down steaming plates of instant noodles when we bounded home from play.

But slowly, when the scent of her skin faded in the air around us, the memory of every minutia took root. The way she flipped the pages of our notebooks and coaxed cursive writing from our fingers, the way her palms gauged the warmth of our foreheads and nursed us back to mischief. We fidgeted with spinners she surprise-gifted us, stroked the scrapes that her kisses had dissolved, revised the sums she'd drilled into our heads. She recited folktales every night before bed, pecked us on the nose, lobbed back every question we volleyed at her from dawn until midnight, and trained us to wield the strings of a guitar. We mused over how she emptied medicine cups filled with sweet syrups into our mouths, squeezed our hands when the syringe needle stabbed our skins.

Then we marveled that she hadn't fled our clutches even earlier.

Thomas Mantz, *Church*

Glenis Moore

Glenis has been writing since the first UK Covid lockdown
and does her writing at night as she suffers from severe
insomnia. When she is not writing she makes beaded
jewellery, reads, cycles and sometimes runs 10K races slowly.
She lives, with her long-suffering partner and three cats, just
outside Cambridge in the flat expanse of the Fens, UK.

Dark

I am afraid of the dark.
The rustling and cracking of twigs,
the shrouded figures of trees
lurking just out of focus,
with murderous intentions,
the sudden whoosh of a bat
or bird disturbed by your footsteps,
the dank smell of cold even in a summer mist,
and the slight brush of something
you cannot see
even when touched by the lights
of an approaching car.
And yet I walked three miles that night
to be with you. I did not know then
that your love was a darkness
I would never escape from.

James B. Nicola

James B. Nicola is the author of eight collections of poetry, the latest three being *Fires of Heaven: Poems of Faith and Sense, Turns & Twists,* and *Natural Tendencies.* His nonfiction book *Playing the Audience: The Practical Actor's Guide to Live Performance* won a Choice Magazine Award. He has received a Dana Literary Award, two Willow Review Awards, Storyteller's People's Choice Award, one Best of the Net, one Rhysling, and eleven Pushcart nominations—for which he feels stunned and grateful. A graduate of Yale, James hosts the Writers' Roundtable at his library branch in Manhattan: walk-ins are always welcome.

Knells and Bells

A knell of death
fades smoothly
into silence

and grief gives rise
to gratitude
once more

The ring of truth
may die
but not the hope

that one day
some brave soul
shall clang again

Without
the celebrations
and the cycles

all would only
be
unbearable

Michael Moreth, *Haute-Monde*

Ihor Pidhainy

Born in Canada, Ihor Pidhainy is a teacher and writer based in Atlanta. His poetry can be seen this summer in *Washington Square Review*, *Quarry Press*, *Pause Press Pause*, *Scapegoat Review* and elsewhere. He has two chapbooks—*Meditations on Fathers and Sons* (Bottlecap Press) and *Snowball* (Origami Press).

Fantasia Returned

I wonder what it'd be like
Born in another age
Amongst a foreign tribe
Perhaps to be present before this oh so familiar stranger
And to see her shining eyes
Shine on me unshod
Of life's heavy iron shoes

In the court I am told that I hold the post of Fool.
So I am a Fool—
If my utterance brings down a kingdom.
I'm glib with tongue
And can fit a thing to a name—
You blush, world weary
You curse, iron-jawed sailors' troubadours

This age is dishonest
These sages faux
This is an old story I'm retelling, paraphrasing, plagiarizing

Let us turn
To this Kingdom by the sea
Where gentle cliffs mock comely clouds
Where leaping to your death
Is commenced, sight unseen—

Float instead to where you wish.
Our tribe is quite polite
We are chivalrous and gallant
We boat the learned and the wise.
We are mounted in divinity
And flourish in emptiness.
Sharing a thoughtful waltz
Making motion with our feet
Mouthing facts and truths
Who can see one's heart—
Dancing, dancing, turning.
It is by this poet's words that lies are bought.

Kenneth Pobo

Kenneth Pobo (he/him) is the author of twenty-one chapbooks and nine full-length collections. Recent books include *Bend of Quiet* (Blue Light Press), *Loplop in a Red City* (Circling Rivers), and most recently, *At The Window, Silence* (Fernwood Press). His work has appeared in *Asheville Poetry Review, North Dakota Quarterly, Amsterdam Quarterly, Nimrod, Mudfish, Hawaii Review*, and elsewhere.

I'm Alive

but I forgot about it.
I breathe and eat
While a violet raises
her eye to see
a growing red
zinnia. Each day isn't

a gift or a curse. It's
the moment when
the tennis ball may
or may not make it over

the net. Growing up
(which century was that?)
I was told that my goal
should be a full life.
Full of what?
Zest and vigor?
Both wear me out. Or
getting a massage
from a warm spring sun
and falling asleep?

I feel my pulse. Yup,
I'm still here,
on our muddy porch
listening to birds
fight despite
a full feeder.

Provocateur

When Lenny says
at the town hall meeting
"LGBTQ are fully human"
a rumble of mumble
drifts across the room.
Some guy gets up and says
"They are not."

Lenny worries that someone
may have a gun.
The odds are good.

Mayor Caln pounds the gavel,
says "We must move along."

Move along—
to stand in the same place.

Edward Lee, *Flight of Days*

Helen Rana

Helen is a member of the Writers' Guild of Great Britain and was a Creative Writing Associate at Bath Spa University in 2017-21. Her short stories have been published in anthologies, and her eight full-length and eight short screenplays have all been selected for film festivals or won awards.

The Foundling

Justin asked the wrong question.

He had already left for the office that morning. I was trying to forgive him for last year's affair with a colleague and trying to forget how glamorous she looked on social media. Beautiful, slim, Indian, elegant.

Ready for work, I opened our front door. A wicker bag was on the doorstep. Not expecting a delivery, I looked inside. A newborn baby, swaddled up in a blanket. I recoiled, searching urgently all around. People walking to the bus stop, drivers, cyclists, the usual rush hour motion. Nobody who looked like they had just dumped a baby. My heart racing, I took some deep breaths, dialled 999 and described the situation.

'Is the baby safe and well?'

It hadn't moved. I was suddenly struck with dread that it might be dead. I bent down and touched its cheek.

The relief of warm skin.

The policewoman carried on. 'Have you taken Baby indoors? Given them a little cuddle?'

'It's asleep. I haven't touched it.'

I reddened. Despite all my professional and materialistic success, I had no idea how to handle an infant.

'OK. Our officers will be with you shortly.'

'Thanks, bye.'

I hesitated uncertainly on our threshold, then carried the basket gingerly by its thick handles inside the house. I placed it on the kitchen table, careful not to wake the child. I wouldn't know what to do if it started crying.

The room was the same but their air in it had changed.

I phoned Justin. 'You'll never guess what, someone's abandoned a baby outside our house.'

The baby's brown eyes opened, looked up, appraised me, unimpressed. I hoped the police would get here soon.

Justin was silent for a very long time.

Eventually he asked, 'Does it look a bit Indian?'

Wrong question.

Rehumanized

"Thank you for taking the time to meet with me today," said the sociologist that cold afternoon. She wanted to chat for free, but I told her she'd have to pay for my attention like everybody else. I was living and working on the streets. Time was money.

We reached a compromise where she bought me a meal and I talked. It was a luxury to sit down somewhere warm with a person who was not a threat. She said she couldn't pay me, for research ethics reasons, but could buy me food and a hot drink. She was investigating why others 'end up' as prostitutes, although I corrected her about that. It's not the end for most of us, just a difficult moment in a changeable life.

"An interregnum," she called it. She had all the right words.

Her questions were stupid. Why does anybody sell sexual services? Obviously because we are poor people in a tough situation, desperate for money. Clients pay us to follow their orders. It's simple supply and demand. Power and money. Need and want. You wouldn't think it would take three years at uni to work that out.

She was calling her thesis 'Dehumanisation' because she said that punters don't think prostitutes count as people. They see us as facilities to be used, dominated, discarded. Like public toilets or parking spaces. She was right about that. People like us don't count.

Then Covid-19 came along, and officials suddenly started counting who was living on the streets. Every single individual. Overnight I became a problem that needed to be solved, an item added to someone's to do list. They had to quickly get us off the streets, help us, treat us like real people. I was given a bed, a room, food and safety. For a short while I was rehumanised.

Just for another interregnum.

It didn't last long of course. The virus left, life went back to normal, I'm back on the streets.

Uncounted again.

Re-

-dehumanised.

Camellia Paul, Flower in My Eyes

Philip Eric Repko

Philip E. Repko is a sixty-three-year-old Pop-Pop, dad,
husband, and purveyor of poetry and prose. Professionally,
he has held down the educational fort for more than 40 years.
In November of 2024, Phil published his first book of poetry,
Pieces of April, through Anxiety Press. It is available at
Amazon and other online vendors. Reviews suggest that if
you want poetry to prompt you to deeply think - and feel -
here is a place to start.

Disencumbrance

This next step will test my mettle
in that it demands belief in miracles.
Those who love and care for me,
(and also those who scoff and sneer)
agree in principle with one detail:
I alone have forged this chain.

But now these goodly people,
within whom I have thrown my lot,
contend that I may separate
my weakness from myself—
by gesture and intent,
allow the power outside me
to gather up the chaff
and leave me as the whole and healthy grain.

I do humbly confess I am not sure.
Of course, I would slough off the heavy cloak,
to leave transgressions lying in the road.
My reconciliation stalls, because,
though I am penitent for all my sins;

acknowledge ownership for every fault;
I find it hard to think I can cast off
within a time as brief as months or years,
the coarse and heavy sediment I've caught.

What force or power pulses so with love
and care that it will gladly bear the weight
of self-destructive choices one-by-one,
accumulated error and of clout?
Of course, again, I never stand to know
the answer to that question—It is faith
alone can make me take the fateful step.
I'm done with Hamlet! Wish me well. I go.

Paris Rosemont

Paris Rosemont is an Asian-Australian poet with a niche in theatrical performance poetry. Her debut poetry collection *Banana Girl* (WestWords, 2023) was shortlisted by the Association for the Study of Australian Literature for the 2024 Mary Gilmore Award. *Banana Girl* was also shortlisted for Poetry Book Awards 2024 in Australia, Greece and the UK, and awarded Distinguished Favorite in the NYC Independent Press Award 2025 (USA). Paris's second poetry collection, *Barefoot Poetess*, was released in April 2025. She may be found on Instagram @msparisrose.

Endangered 7

---

they are rarely seen —
nymphs running with wolves, skinny
dipping with selkies

a secret grotto
where they lay their scene glimmers
vast as time itself

moon-dippers shucking
societal shells – bathing
in new-found freedom

milky skin – salt laced
sea converge orgiastic
with unfettered joy

elixir of truth –
they remember gaia. they
remember themselves

I dream of your ears
backlit by the glow of dawn
as I spoon you without touching.
It is summer and we are clammy, sundering
ourselves from the slickness of night's binds.
Side by side we air ourselves like strips of jerky
drying off. We don't have the air conditioner
cranking cool enough. Two days and a thousand
miles later, you tell me you are burning up
with a fever. *Is it love, you ask the doctor*
you don't actually go to see. In this
moment as I watch
sunrise turn the
apricot question
mark of your ear
almost translucent
I trail my finger
lightly along
the curve & dip
of your sleeping
body like a cello
resting, and the
world unfolds: a
Spiegel im Spiegel.
I inch a little closer
my breasts nudging
into your back as you
stir and tuck my arm
under the wing of yours.
The even motor of your
breaths tell me you have
returned to your dreams.
I don't need to fall asleep
to return to mine.

Mary Ellen Shaughan

Mary Ellen Shaughan is a native Iowan who now calls
Western Massachusetts home. Her poetry has appeared in
Foliate Oak, Gyroscope Review, Califragile, Amethyst Review, Page &
Spine, Blue Moon, 2River View, Skipjack Review, and others. Her
first collection of poetry, *Home Grown,* is available online
through Amazon, Barnes & Noble and elsewhere.

Center Aisle, Fourth Pew from the Rear

She felt like a stranger in their midst,
an imposter in that house of worship.
The words, both read and spoken,
were familiar to her ears
she remembered when they
had cheered her,
inspired her, allayed her fears.

She recalled her earlier piety,
wondering where and when
she had lost it, surprised
at how little she missed it.

Now she stood when
the congregants stood
knelt when they knelt
sat when they sat.

While others filed forward to
receive wafer and wine, she remained
seated, noting their eagerness to
be among the first to reach the altar

as if there were a limited
supply of the sacraments
and also something about the early bird.

Camellia Paul, *Princess*

R.P. Singletary

A rural native of the southeastern U.S.A., R. P. Singletary writes fiction, drama, poetry, hybrid. Pub'd in *Litro, BULL, Rathalla Review, The Rumen, Wasteland Review, EBB - Ukraine, Jonah, Ancient Paths, Wicked Gay Ways, Screen Door Review, Bending Genres, Pink Disco, The Ana,* and elsewhere. Visit him at www.rpsingletary.com.

Memory out of habit / *Picture with no words*

You remember that photograph I told you about, the one I didn't get to snap? In that New York blizzard, right after first of the year? I was running late, that conference, one of those grand hotel complexes. Midtown, my hands covered in Arctic gloves, my phone thawing in my pocket. Behatted and enscarfed, no less—

I DIDN'T WANT TO EXPOSE MYSELF AND RISK, what?, GETTING COLD.

That all went through my head when I saw this, what I keep seeing:

> In a quiet of a one-way, west-bound, tree-lined, gentrifying Helluva Kitchen's street, a lone young beautiful nun **tip-toes** awkwardly, silently naturally silently, it being the literal dead of Northern winter
>
> **emerges** pre-Dawn **etches** faintest, unknown-sourced light, sleeping chamber north side of street,

hikes her slender yet profound, proud black-robed
self,

high-steps round mounds of fresh plowed,
            down since midnight,
            as if in its own habit-- valued,

flees to God
(or within the south-side church where she works??).

<u>I, myself, act not yet out of habit:</u>
Gone
In the short seconds
It would've taken me
To snap her into
pieces, a memory

Jonathan Ukah

Jonathan Chibuike Ukah is a Pushcart Prize-nominated poet who lives in the UK with his family. His poems have been featured in the *Atticus Review, San Antonio Review, The Ephemeral Literary Review, Strange Horizons, The Pierian, The Unleash Lit* and elsewhere. He is the winner of the Alexander Pope Poetry Award 2023 and the second runner-up of the Wingless Dreamer Publishing Poetry Prize 2023.

The Night I Saw the Moon

My sister took me to the middle of the forest,
into the circle where two people met
to find out if they knitted together
like the thread and the torn cloth,
to gaze at the moon when it emerged.
We slid into the shadows like fading daffodils,
and the night stretched out a short sleeve,
invited me to slug my amputated arm in.
I turned my scarred face to the dark sky,
flushed out my blood tongue like tired petals;
my tired eyes shut down like a broken clock,
my charred face mixed with the darkness
because there was no moonlight.
My sister and I waited for half an hour,
alone in the middle of the wilderness,
like two people ostracised from their kindred
for a crime against the gods of their land;
only a drop of frozen dews trickled on my tongue,
down to my jutting jaw and naked neck.
There was no moon appointed to shine tonight.
The following day, the moon staggered to us
like a scanty bone tossed at a hungry wild dog.

I asked the moon why it stayed away.
"Did you not see the clammy fingers of darkness?"
I could not believe that the moon asked me that.
"When the scorpion refuses to act like one,
the children will lift it like a tardy rope."

Michael Moreth, *Impeccant*

VISUAL ARTIST INFORMATION

Lis Anna-Langston

Hailed as "an author with a genuine flair for originality" by Midwest Book Review and "a loveable, engaging, original voice…" by Publishers Weekly, Lis Anna-Langston is the author of five novels. Raised along the winding current of the Mississippi River she studied Literature and Creative Writing and graduated Magna Cum Laude in 2023. Winner of the NYC Big Book Award, Independent Press Awards and dozens of other book awards, she is a three-time Pushcart Prize nominee, with work published extensively in literary journals.

Wesley R. Bishop

Wesley R. Bishop is a professor, poet, and editor in northeast Alabama. He is the co-author of *Liberating Fat Bodies: Social Media Censorship and Body Size Activism.* He is currently working on a visual art series about fat people at peace. He is the managing editor at North Meridian Press.

Lisa Dailey

Lisa Dailey is a mixed-media artist, author, and adventurer. Her artwork blends painting, photography, and embroidery, creating richly textured pieces inspired by nature's smallest, often-overlooked details. Committed to sustainability, she incorporates recycled materials into her work, giving new life to discarded items through art. A third-generation photographer, Lisa's deep appreciation for the natural world also shapes her writing. Her memoir, *Square Up*, chronicles a year-long journey around the world and her personal journey through grief. Originally from Montana, she now finds inspiration nestled between the mountains and the ocean in Bellingham, Washington.

Edward Lee

Edward Lee's poetry, short stories, non-fiction and photography have been published in magazines in Ireland, England and America, including *The Stinging Fly, Skylight 47, Acumen, The Blue Nib and Poetry Wales*. He is currently working on a novel. He also makes musical noise under the names Ayahuasca Collective, Orson Carroll, Lego Figures Fighting, and Pale Blond Boy.

Thomas Mantz

Active since 2019, Thomas Mantz is a photographer capturing the world in 120mm and 35mm.

Michael Moreth

Michael Moreth is a recovering Chicagoan living in the rural, micropolitan City of Sterling, the Paris of Northwest Illinois.

Camellia Paul

Camellia Paul has a Masters in Comparative Literature from Jadavpur University, India. She works as a Senior Instructional Designer in a multinational ed-tech company. Her works of translation, fiction, poetry, and art regularly appear in magazines, online journals, and anthologies. Camellia loves owls, nature, reading, listening to music, and exploring cultures.

Edward Michael Supranowicz

Edward Michael Supranowicz is the grandson of Irish and Russian/Ukrainian immigrants. He grew up on a small farm in Appalachia. He has a grad background in painting and printmaking. Some of his artwork has recently or will soon appear in *Fish Food, Streetlight, Another Chicago Magazine, The Door Is a Jar, The Phoenix*, and other journals. Edward is also a published poet who has been nominated for the Pushcart Prize multiple times.

Claudia Tong

Claudia is an artist and quantitative researcher based in London, creating at the intersection of physical and digital art. Her practice spans from paintings and illustrations to mixed media, visual computing and music. With a background in computer science and psychology, she has worked, lived and exhibited internationally.

www.ingramcontent.com/pod-product-compliance
Lightning Source LLC
Chambersburg PA
CBHW071132100726
47908CB00008B/2582